THE SIN EATERS

A HOPE SZE MEDICAL CRIME STORY AND TRUE CRIME ESSAY

MELISSA YI

CONTENTS

The Sin Eaters 1
The Heroes in the Shadows 25

Afterword 39
About the Author 41
Also by Melissa Yi 42

Join Melissa's mailing list at www.melissayuaninnes.com

"The Sin Eaters" originally published in Montreal Noir

Published by Olo Books in association with Windtree Press

Cover photo by Alexandr Ivanov | Pixabay

The photo does not literally represent the characters in the story.

Yi, Melissa, author Blue Christmas / Melissa Yi.
Issued in print (978-1-927341-83-4) and electronic (ISBN 978-1-927341-79-7) formats.

To advise of typographical errors, please contact olobooks@gmail.com

THE SIN EATERS

I don't trust guys who are too good-looking.

Strange, since I was sitting to the right of a rather fantastic-looking patient at that moment. He had carefully-tousled dirty-blond hair, high cheekbones, and very white skin.

The patient perched on the edge of the bed with his legs and his hands crossed, gazing steadily at the plastic surgeon.

Dr. Mendelson didn't seem to notice. He waved at me and told the patient, "This is Hope Sze. She's a resident doctor, but she won't bother you." The doctor flipped through the patient's chart and grunted. "You're healing well. Lift your chin up." He glanced at the chart's "before" pictures.

I peered over his shoulder, trying not to make any noise. Canada's health care system doesn't pay for aesthetic surgery, so these patients fork out of their own pockets and don't expect a zillion little students descending upon them. Dr. Mendelson had said that I could follow him around his morning clinic at Montreal's Jewish Hospital if I promised not to touch anyone, speak, or practically breathe around the white walls and stainless steel sinks.

This patient's picture and present-day look didn't seem all that different to me. He'd paid for cheek implants and Botox, even though he was only 22 years old, or five years younger than me. The implants did give a fox-like sharpness to his features that I thought was kind of unnecessary when his green eyes fixated on me in an uncomfortable way. But mostly, he watched Dr. Mendelson, a little gnome of a guy with a deeply furrowed brow and a rumpled lab coat, who was observing him right back.

Dr. Mendelson took another picture and said, "Could you stand by the window? The light is better."

The patient posed with such alacrity, I figured he was either a model or a wannabe. Dr. Mendelson snapped some frontal and side pictures, and the patient leaned forward to check his own image on the back of the SLR camera.

"That's the best one," the patient said, pointing a thin, pale-skinned finger at a picture of himself almost glaring at the camera with that screw-you image that most ads project. "Can I get a copy? You can e-mail it to me, or put it on Tumblr." His voice was high and thin, not as striking as his appearance. He was also on the skinny side, although his skin looked better under natural light than fluorescent.

I wondered what he did for money so that he could afford plastic surgery at the age of 22. Or maybe it was the Bank of Mom and Dad.

I really wanted to ask him about his work. Because I was forbidden to speak, I glanced at his chart. His name was Raymond Pascal Gusarov. He was a Scorpio like me, not that it mattered, but we'd both recently had our birthdays. In fact —I took a quick look—he'd had surgery *on* his birthday,

November second, which seemed a little weird to me. *Yay, I turned 22. Better have someone cut my face open.*

Then again, I've never been a big fan of plastic surgery. I keep hoping that my Asian genes will protect me a little from the ravages of time.

"I don't put patient photos online because of patient confidentiality," said Dr. Mendelson, scribbling in the chart without looking up.

"I want it," said Raymond Pascal Gusarov in a way that made me think he wasn't used to being denied.

Dr. Mendelson grunted. "I'll have copies made and leave them with my secretary."

"At least 300 pixels, so I can print them," said Gusarov.

"Only the best for you," said Dr. Mendelson, still without bothering to make eye contact. He held the oak door open for me and told Raymond, "You can pay the secretary for them when you pick them up."

Gusarov cut ahead of me and offered the doctor his hand. "Thank you, Dr. Mendelson. I appreciate it."

Dr. Mendelson squinted at him. The light blinked off his glasses for a moment before he shook the patient's hand. "My pleasure." Then Dr. M waved me through the opening ahead of Gusarov, and I hurried through, because if the doctor's asking you to do something, you look extra weak if you let a patient beat you to it. Twice.

The thought of Raymond Pascal Gusarov nagged at me for the rest of the clinic. I didn't know why. Most of the aesthetic patients were trim and fit and obviously very conscious of their looks. When Dr. Mendelson asked one mother of a pre-schooler and a 20-month-old if she weighed a hundred pounds, she sniffed and said, "Please! Ninety-five!" I don't think I've weighed under 100 pounds for the past ten years, and I'm pretty fine-boned.

But Raymond Pascal Gusarov's fox face seemed to follow me home as I hurried down Côte-des-Neiges, past St. Joseph's Hospital. Even though I was surrounded by people spilling off the blue and white STCUM buses with groceries hooked on their arms, and some eager businesses had started hanging tinsel and Christmas lights, I found myself checking over my shoulder and deliberately ignoring the Notre-Dame-des-Neiges Cemetery as I turned right and huffed myself halfway up the hill to my latest apartment. My grandmother really, really hates that my new address overlooks a graveyard, despite my fancier digs and real, live security guard.

I felt slightly better after I locked the door behind me, but as soon as I kicked off my boots and dropped my backpack on the hardwood floor, I Googled Raymond Pascal Gusarov. He came up right away. Kind of an usual name, I guess.

The same green eyes stared out at me from a dozen different photos. Some of them were black and white, most of them colour, nearly all of them professional or not far off. He looked younger in some of them, with a rounder face. Less fox, more chicken. But he never looked innocent.

He was on Twitter and Facebook and all the usual suspects. He had a fan page on Facebook with only 77 likes. I know that's probably more than any page I'd ever host, but from our brief encounter, I figured it would really bother Raymond Pascal Gusarov that he wasn't more popular.

Some people have a very strong sense of self. They're happy, they're confident, and they don't need a million Google hits to reassure them that they exist. Many doctors and nurses are like that. But not this guy.

I scrolled through his fan page. He posted one to three times a day: pictures of himself, videos of himself, little messages that I didn't want to think too much about, like "I'M DOWNTOWN, BITCHESS!!!! Cum & C me."

My phone buzzed with a message from Ryan Wu: *What's up?* I had to smile. Ryan had just given me the world's most beautiful iPhone for my birthday, and I couldn't look at it or touch it without thinking of him. Which was probably what he had in mind.

I texted back, *I'm looking something up.*

Work?

Sort of. I didn't want to text any more, because I'd recently caught my third murderer—maybe three-and-a-half killers, if you want to get technical about it—and Ryan thinks that I should hightail it out of Montreal and join him in dull but safe Ottawa. The man had a point.

Ryan promptly called me instead. I rolled my eyes before I tapped the green key to answer the phone. He knew me too well. "Hey, babe."

"Are you on another case?"

"Um. Not officially."

His voice tightened. "You were going to avoid those."

I didn't answer for a second.

"Right?" said Ryan.

"I'm just ... looking something up on the computer. I'm not getting strangled or anything like that."

"For once," he muttered, which I chose to ignore. "What are you looking up?"

I couldn't tell him without breaking patient confidentiality, but Ryan is a computer whiz. He could be so useful on this. "Let's say that I have someone that I want to look up. Online. So I'm not going to tango with a killer. I just need more information."

"What have you got right now?"

"Some Google images, Facebook, and Twitter. Plus a pretty website with some contact information."

"What are you looking for?"

"I don't know," I admitted. "It just feels ... fishy to me."

"You want me to do it?"

"I can't tell you his name."

"Okay. So what do you want to know?"

"I want to know more about this guy. I want to know where he lives, and if he's doing anything else that's questionable."

I could practically feel him thinking through the phone. Ryan has a fairly massive brain, not to mention a long, lean runner's build, and ... don't get me started. He said, "You might try looking at the Exif."

"What's that?"

"The Exchangable Image File Format. I'll send you some information about it. People only think about stuff like 'Is this a JPG?' but the Exif not only stores the file format, it tells you the time, date and GPS."

Uh oh. You mean you could Snapchat a naughty picture of yourself and freaks could figure out where you lived? Too much scary to process right now. I also ignored the niggling voice at the back of my head saying, *Isn't this an invasion of privacy? Are you violating the Hippocratic Oath? Huh, freak?*

Instead, I scanned and clicked various articles that Ryan sent me and asked, "Me doing this isn't illegal, though, right?"

He laughed. "How is information illegal?"

Oh, Ryan. He was so innocent sometimes. I let that one pass, and told him I couldn't wait until I saw him on Sunday, before we hung up. Long distance relationships plus on-call schedules officially suck.

I've never been a huge computer person. I like them, I

use them, but I can't make them sit up and purr the way Ryan does. So I was pretty excited when I started tracking down his locations—mostly downtown and East Montreal, a few in the Plateau. Never my neighbourhood of Côte-des-Neiges. Phew. Because of its three hospitals and one university, my hood's got "a lot of students and immigrants," as Mireille, another resident, put it, but obviously not a big draw, bitches.

Speaking of which, I turned back to Raymond Pascal Gusarov's social media accounts. Most of them repeated the same pics and videos over and over, but I clicked on a few links he'd recommended, that recommended other links, that recommended still more links, mostly posts by TearsOfAClown and Heart's Blood.

TearsOfAClown had posted pictures of gerbils, hamsters, and other fuzzy animals. Strange. I would've guessed that Raymond Pascal Gusarov didn't love other living things as much as himself. Maybe I was totally wrong about him.

Except TearsOfAClown started posting more photos. One hamster was clearly dead, its little body lying stiffly on its side.

In the next photo, another hamster posed with a tiny chainsaw over the dead hamster.

My heart thudded. What the heck? Was this Photoshop? I couldn't tell. I've got no skills that way.

In the third photo, the dead hamster had been decapitated. Its small, golden head was sitting on the ground, severed side down, eyes still closed, while the chainsaw hamster stood above it, wearing a miniature face mask.

More photos. More decapitated hamsters. The murdering hamster seemed to wink as it held its little chainsaw aloft.

Some of those hamsters, I'm pretty sure, had been alive up until the moment their necks had been cut.

Oh. Em. Gee.

What could I do about this? I thought this guy was as nutballs as you could get, but could we arrest him for cruelty to animals?

So far, I'd only put away people who'd killed other people. I could call the Humane Society, of course, but what if he said the animals were already dead? What if he claimed it was art?

I felt sick. Before med school, my literature class had read "The Sin Eater," by Margaret Atwood, where she basically compared modern doctors to 18th century sin eaters, who used to consume food and drink placed on a deceased body, theoretically absorbing the dead's sins so that he or she could ascend to heaven while the sin eater got a square meal. For a few days, I wandered around thinking, *Atwood's right; why am I applying to med school, anyway?*

Finally, I decided, *So what. Sins are interesting*. I made my peace with it. But sometimes I wondered, especially when I ended up confronting this level of insanity. Not only was I taking in the sins of the sick, but I was actively seeking out deranged murderers. Sins cubed.

I took a deep breath. My phone buzzed again. This time, it was my gentleman in waiting, Dr. John Tucker: *yo yo yo*

Hi, I wrote back. If I ever needed Tucker's silliness, it was now. Even though talking to him on my iPhone vaguely seemed like cheating. Again, maybe that was Ryan's point, since there was little love lost between him and Tucker.

What's wrong?

Again, Tucker seemed to know me too well. How could he tell, through a text? *I'm looking at something disturbing.*

Ryan? JK.

I rolled my eyes, as if he could see me in my white-walled apartment.

Are you on another case?

Slowly, I tapped out the word *Maybe.*

I'm coming over.

You are not. I need to think. 'Bye

I turned my phone to airplane mode, so that neither of my guys could distract me, and started Googling animal cruelty in Montreal. Then I called the humane society for the city. They took my name and number, but when I said I was calling about photos online, I could feel the guy's interest dimming. "Hamsters? In a picture? Okay."

"I know it doesn't sound like much, but I really think we should look into this."

He sighed. "I would love to look into everything, Ms. Sze." He pronounced it See, which was close enough for now. "But we got a report of a guy beating his dog to death. We have to close down a puppy mill in another part of the city. And did you hear about le Berger de l'Étoile?"

I hadn't.

He sighed again. He sounded pretty wrecked, so I thanked him and hung up. Poor guy. It seemed like the animal welfare system was as underfunded as the Montreal medical system. Or worse.

I looked up le Berger de l'Étoile, which turned out to be a for-profit shelter that killed 80 to 200 animals a day. To save money, instead of hiring a veterinarian or an animal health care technician, they had a maintenance worker use the outmoded technique of intracardiac injections, ineptly. So the worker would have to inject up to twelve times, and even then, they'd basically throw the animals in the garbage, still alive.

I covered my eyes. I was heading down a rabbit hole here. I had to concentrate on Raymond Pascal Gusarov.

I Skyped Ryan, who picked up right away. I had to smile at his blurry, pixelated photo from his webcam before I got down to business. "Ry, I've got pictures and I'm sending you the link. I need you to help me figure out if the pictures are real, who did them, and if we can sic the SPCA on him." I figured I could bring Ryan in because the pictures were public, and I didn't know how to prove they were from Raymond Pascal Gusarov.

"On it. Ugh," he said, clicking away, and then he choked on his coffee.

"Sorry, babe." I hated to rope him into this, too, making him into a sin eater when he could work with nice, neat computers all day.

He waved my words away. "Let me see. Okay. I need an IP address...okay, that's interesting."

"What?"

"His IP is 1.2.3.4. Obviously a fake. There's nothing there."

"So ... he covered up his IP address?"

"Pretty much. Let me see what I can do."

While he worked his techno-magic, I busied myself combing through Gusarov's other alias, Heart's Blood, where he wrote stories about screwing other guys, slitting their throats, and eating their hearts. Dear lord. I rubbed my eyes.

Ryan said, "Holy crap. He's using proxies here, bouncing from China to Sweden. Do you have a video?"

My heart was still pounding from Heart's Blood. "Um, I'll see if I can find one."

"Never mind, I'm on it. Videos are nice because they take

up more bandwidth. YouTube won't give out an IP without a police warrant, but ... "

I wondered how he knew that. It was easier to wonder if Ryan was the Chinese Christian golden boy he pretended than to think about what I'd just read.

"I pinged some of my friends. One of them commented on the background for the flying hamster. See how there's a street lamp outside? It's got an unusual shape."

I squinted. It was especially blurry through Skype, but yes, one shot was of a hamster in a cape, in front of a window, with toothpicks through the eyes.

My own eyeballs smarted. *Cannot unsee.* I needed a drink of water, but first, I had to ask, "How long's it going to take you?"

"It takes as long as it takes, Hope. It's not like TV."

"Too bad," I muttered.

Ryan's face stilled. "He's in Montreal. Those street lamps ... my friend found a match on Mapzest."

"I know."

"Is it that patient you were talking about?"

I didn't answer, which was probably enough of an answer.

"Be careful, Hope."

I heard a knock at my apartment door, and jumped. No one should be able to knock on my door since I moved into an apartment with a security guard, unlike the unlocked doors of Mimosa Manor.

I stifled a scream.

Ryan said, "Don't answer it."

"I won't," I said, truly freaked out. Was it possible that while we searched for Raymond Pascal Gusarov, he was tracking us? Was that how he got money for plastic surgery, at the age of 22? Was he some sort of hamster-killing, human heart-eating computer genius?

His before and after pictures weren't too impressive, but what if he'd started out as someone who looked very different, one plastic surgery at a time?

"I'm going to stay on," said Ryan. "If anyone breaks in, I'll call the Montreal police."

Virtual backup. Good. Better than no backup.

I'd put the chain on my door, but I called down to the security desk first. "Hi, this is Hope Sze in apartment 8828. Did you let someone in the building who came up to the eighth floor? I didn't buzz anyone in."

"A man got buzzed into the 23rd floor."

Shit. Of course, there was no stopping him from making his way to my apartment from another floor. Some idiot could have buzzed him in, and then Raymond Pascal Gusarov could decide, *Nope, I'm heading over to kill the detective doctor instead.*

I'd gotten complacent, living in a prettier place. A killer is a killer is a killer.

"What did the man look like?"

"Caucasian, about five nine, blond hair, slim build, jeans and a navy jacket. Is there a problem? Do you need me to come upstairs?"

Someone knocked on the door again, harder this time. I squeaked.

The guard said, "I'll need someone to man the front door. Let me call someone in."

While he did that, Raymond Pascal Gusarov could smash his way in.

"You want me to call the cops?" said Ryan.

A man spoke through the door. "Hope, I know you're in there. Let me in."

My heart seemed to pause for a moment. I recognized this voice, deep in my marrow. I unlocked my lips. "Tucker?"

"Are you okay? You weren't answering your phone, so I got Mireille to let me in. What's going on?"

I let my breath out slowly. He was talking loudly enough that Ryan said, "Is that Tucker?"

I nodded and told Ryan, "You don't need to call the police. But you may need to beat some manners into him."

"Will do," said Ryan, his lips pressed into a grim line, even through the webcam. He didn't offer to hang up, and I didn't ask him to. Tucker and I shouldn't be doing anything that couldn't be witnessed in public, unless people minded Public Displays of Aggravation.

I looked through the keyhole, and sure enough, Tucker stared back at me. Even through the fishbowl of the keyhole lens, distorting the sharp planes of his face, I couldn't help admiring his intelligent brown eyes and yep, that stupid blond hair that he likes to spike with hair gel. "Are you alone?" I said through the door.

"No. I'm with you. There's just this door between us."

I undid the chain and swung the door open, although I still peered behind him. "You scared the hell out of me."

"You didn't answer your phone or e-mail."

"I was busy."

He glanced behind me at my computer, and saw Ryan. "I can see that. Hey, man."

They nodded at each other.

I felt like stamping my feet. This was not the time for civility. I wanted to kick Tucker's ass, no matter how attractive it looked in his dark wash jeans. He pulled off his jacket and threw it on my futon, making himself at home. At least Tucker didn't try to kiss me hello on both cheeks in front of

Ryan, especially while I informed Dr. T, "When I say don't come ... "

"You know that's like waving a red flag in front of me. Strong like bull."

"That's a myth, about bulls and red flag," I said, distracted for a second. "They're colour-blind. They just don't like the movement, especially when the matador is spearing them."

"I know that," said Tucker, and added something in another language, one of his quirks that I wasn't going to respond to right now. He'd basically like to learn every language on the planet. But then he proceeded to translate, "'Talking about bulls is not the same thing as being in the bullring.' What's this case you got?"

I suddenly realized that I might be able to share some of the details with Tucker that I couldn't give Ryan, since Ryan was a civilian. But Tucker couldn't do any of the computer wizardry. I kind of needed both of them.

Shoot.

I ran my hands through my hair in irritation. I'd started growing it out to shoulder length because I hadn't had time to get a haircut. It was starting to get that blobby look, because my hair was so thick that growing out a bob is an exercise in disaster, but I caught Tucker watching me with a speculative cast to his face, his eyes arrested by the movement in of my hands and my hair, not to mention a quick peek down at my chest.

I lowered my arms and immediately glanced at Ryan, whose narrowed eyes shifted between me and Tucker.

As my Jewish patients would say, Oy oy oy oy oy.

Oy.

Back to the case. I cleared my throat and explained, as best I could, that I'd met a creepy patient who was probably posting pictures of decapitated hamsters, but the animal welfare groups in Montreal were overwhelmed.

"Dr. Hope to the rescue, champion of animals and small children," said Tucker.

I wasn't in the mood for sarcasm. "You have a problem with that? Leave."

He glanced at me, surprised. "No, I like animals. My family had a dog. And you know what they say is the hallmark of an antisocial personality: fire setting, cruelty to animals, and bedwetting. We'd better catch this guy before he hurts anyone else."

"Hang on a second," said Ryan. "Bedwetting?"

I nodded. "I know it sounds weird, but when they researched sociopaths, they found that they had these three things in common. That's what the research shows. That, and the most important personality trait: a lack of remorse. The average person does something wrong and feels bad. A sociopath might apologize because it's politically expedient, but really, he or she doesn't care."

Ryan cracked his knuckles. It startled me, even though I couldn't hear the noise as well through Skype. He hasn't done that in years. I guess the stress of detective work was getting to him, too. "Okay. Let's get this nut."

Music to my ears.

Ryan doubled down on the computer side. Tucker asked me a few more questions about the patient, and I remembered that he'd considered doing psychiatry before he decided on family medicine. That could come in handy.

"It sounds like he could have body dysmorphic disorder. It's still unusual for any guy to get plastic surgery on his face at any age, let alone 22," Tucker said, his brow pleated in thought. I tried not to register that he looked even more yummy when he was thinking. What can I say? Intelligence is a turn-on, even though he was saying something pretty obvious. He continued, "Maybe he doesn't like the way he looks. Maybe he's trying to change himself."

That was speculative, but I didn't want to interrupt his chain of thought.

"Maybe he's trying to hide himself."

Uh. Now he was getting into woo woo territory, for me, so I was relieved when Ryan said, "Got him. He's online right now, just posted another picture, ughh ... but he didn't manage to cover it up in time. He's close to St. Marc's hospital, on Cote-des-Neiges."

I stiffened. That's my area. The three hospitals in my area are St. Joseph's Hospital, the Jewish Hospital, and St. Marc's, the francophone children's hospital, all within about a 20 minute walk of each other. My old apartment, Mimosa Manor, was basically next door to St. Marc's, as well as across from UQAM, the Université de Québec à Montréal. Fortunately, St. Marc's was now a forty minute walk to my new apartment, but it's all too close to an antisocial animal killer, for my liking. I licked my lips. "Can you give me his address?"

"I can give you his router address."

"Done." I wrote down the numbers and letters on an old-fashioned sheet of paper, then held them up for him to read and double-check.

Ryan nodded. "Now what are you going to do?"

"For once, I'm calling the police."

He sighed in relief. Even Tucker nodded. "I wouldn't go near this guy, if I could help it. Are you doing plastics again tomorrow?"

"No. It was a one-time thing. Dr. Huot let me go because it was my second-last day of palliative care, and now she kind of lets me do what I want." Not to brag, but I'm like the prodigal daughter since my last murder case. For the past two days, she's let me wander from St. Joe's to the Samuel G. Wasserman Jewish Hospital, as long as I'm doing clinical work.

Tucker laughed. "The perks of fame."

"Yeah. I get to do plastic surgery." I glanced at the IP address again. "Thanks, Ryan. I l—" Yikes. I almost told him I loved him, right in front of Tucker, whose dark eyes suddenly bore into me. "I mean, thanks."

"You're welcome." Ryan's webcam image grinned at my slip-up—he knew exactly what I'd been about to say—but not too hard. "You're calling the police right now, right?"

"Yup. Officer Visser. She's cool."

"You'll call me back, after you're done?"

"Yeah. She'll probably need to talk to you anyway, since you're the brains of the organization."

He laughed, but he liked that. I could tell. At least, until Tucker said, "I'll have to be the brawn, then."

Miracle of miracles, Officer Visser was on that night, but she wasn't in the office. I tried to explain it to one of her colleagues, who said he'd give her the message, but he obviously wasn't interested.

Tucker said, "Tough luck," and tried to take my hand, but I shook him off and paced back and forth while Skype reconnected me to Ryan.

"You did all you could, right?" said Ryan. His video froze up for a second before it restarted with his dark, concerned eyes pressing into mine.

"Sure." But I was thinking about that IP address. Could I use it to look up the guy? I know I said I'd never climb back into danger, and I wouldn't, but ...

Ryan's pixelated mouth clamped together. "Don't go there."

I nodded.

"I mean it, Hope. I'll never help you again if you keep endangering yourself. This is enough. Right?" His tone changed, and I realized that he was looking over my shoulder at Tucker now.

Tucker nodded. He stood too close behind me. Another six inches and I could press my shoulder blade against his chest. Tucker said, "I'll keep her on lockdown."

"You will not," I said, shifting away from him and planting my hands on my hips.

They both looked at me.

"You got a death wish?" said Ryan, through the screen on my right. "How many times do you have to run after killers, bare-handed?"

"Some people commit suicide by cop," Tucker agreed, adding to Ryan, "That's when they're too chicken to kill themselves, but they try to provoke an officer into shooting them. But it's like you're trying suicide by sociopath."

I had to think about that for a second. "I'm not. I just can't sit here and do nothing."

"Sure you can," said Tucker, grabbing on to my hand and holding it a little too firmly.

Ryan scowled at both of us.

I withdrew my hand, even though the back part of my brain wanted to curl all of me against all of Tucker. I took an obvious step away from him and said, "Don't worry, I'm not going to screw Tucker while he's holding me prisoner."

"Pity," said Tucker, in a fake British accent that made me laugh.

"Maybe I'll just hang out with you guys for a while," said Ryan, still watching us from the webcam. "Tucker? You following hockey?"

Tucker grinned. "The Habs just killed Phoenix."

Ryan scoffed. "I wouldn't call 3-2 killing them. They had to go to overtime."

"That's part of their charm!"

I stared from one of them to the other and said, in French, "*T'es pas serieux.*"

"Crazy like a Coyote!" said Tucker, which I didn't understand at all, but it must have been a hockey reference, because Ryan said, "Let's see how they do with the Predators, that's all I'm saying."

OMG. My guys were now bonding over hockey. Not that it's an unheard-thing, but in the middle of a case? C'mon. And the fact that neither of them trusted me was even more irritating, if justified. While they talked about men with sticks, I tried to figure out what to do.

The SPCA couldn't help me. The police didn't take me seriously. I only knew one other officer, J. Rivera, who hated my guts. Now what?

I opened up another window on my computer to start researching this. Surely I couldn't be the only person disturbed by an animal abuser. What did other people do?

Traditionally, they went to the media and tried to get the newspaper, radio, and TV outlets interested. But nowadays, it looked like they went online.

So I followed their lead and started a Facebook group. I needed a catchy title.

"What are you doing?" said Tucker.

"Can't talk. Working," I said.

He read over my shoulder. "Help the Hamsters? What?"

"Have you got a better title?" I snapped.

"Sure. Headless hamsters. Help Hammy."

Of course, Ryan wanted to get in on the action and was not impressed. "Do you know what you're doing?"

"I'm trying to do some detection online. That way, I'm not risking my neck. I thought you guys would be thrilled."

Ryan stared at me through the camera and repeated, "Do you know what you're doing?"

"I can set up a Facebook group."

"But then the killer can find *you* through *your* IP address. Haven't you learned anything?"

A chill crept down my back. I stared at him.

He shook his head and said, "I'll do it."

My dummy account got a lot of traffic right away. I was on my phone all the time, and not only researching articles. People wanted to join the Facebook group. People with IT experience, teenagers, whatever. I accepted them all, one at a time, before I realized that this was madness and made it an open group.

The next day, I got a message on Facebook. The subject was "yr group," and the sender was Vladamir Kzurstan, which sounded made up, but when I clicked on it, the message read, *catch me if you can*.

I know there are a lot of wannabes, but could it really be this guy giving himself up? I asked Ryan. He called me and said, "This profile got made two hours ago. It looks like a set up. But you can tell the SPCA and the police anyway, while I try and get more info."

This Internet research was driving me crazy. I had to do something. So, on my last day of palliative care, I asked Dr. Huot if I could return to plastic surgery one more time.

The doctor's eyes twinkled. "Oh, my dear, are you thinking of changing specialties?"

"I'm just going for a visit," I said, not in the mood to joke, and she touched my arm.

"Of course, dear Hope."

Gah. Before she could adorn me with angel wings, I

rushed down Cote-des-Neiges to the Jewish Hospital, wishing I was a simple girl hitting up the ATM and grabbing a bento box, but it couldn't be helped. I had sins to eat.

I hurried back to Dr. Mendelson's clinic. I had no idea if he was in the OR or if he was in clinic, but my luck held. I spotted his rumpled lab coat heading into his office.

I really didn't want to do this. I was trying to be a good resident and not mix my detective work up with my day/night job. But it drove me crazy to spin around on the Internet, trying to build a case, when I thought I knew who the perpetrator was.

I stopped at his secretary and told her I needed a few minutes with Dr. Mendelson.

"You're not on the schedule today," she said, staring at me over the wire rims of her glasses.

"I know. You're right. I just have some ... information about one of his patients," I said.

She sniffed. "I'll see if he'll see you. He's a very busy man."

I crossed my fingers under the desk. Two crucial minutes later, I was sitting in his office. His degrees were hung on the walls, but his desk was covered in an array of old-fashioned books and journals, with barely enough room for a flat screen monitor, keyboard, and the sandwich he was chewing on. He put the sandwich down when he saw me. I thought I smelled liverwurst, which always struck me as something one wouldn't eat willingly.

"What can I do for you?" he said.

Ask not what you can do for me. Ask what you can do for the hamsters, spun through my brain, but I wasn't crazy enough to say so.

"I think one of your patients is torturing animals and may move on to humans," I said.

He choked and coughed, spraying a few crumbs.

I explained to him, using my phone to show him the pictures. His eyes shot up, and he only read a few sentences of Heart's Bleed before he looked at me. "This is a sick man. But what does this have to do with one of my patients?"

"It's Raymond Pascal Gusarov," I said, and his body sagged.

"That one," he said, in a way that made me ask, "What is it?"

"The secretary told me that his credit card bounced. He never paid me for the surgery. And I had those photos made up for him this week, too!"

"Is he coming for the photos?" I asked.

"I left him a message that he couldn't have them until he paid for the surgery. He'll probably never show up again. He has thirty days to pay."

I was thinking about Al Capone. "If he doesn't pay, could you mention it to the police instead of a collection agency?"

Dr. Mendelson stared at me like I was speaking Kurdish.

"You know Al Capone?" I said, which didn't help matters, so I had to explain, "He was the gangster who ordered the St. Valentine's Day Massacre. But they never caught him for that, or bootlegging, or prostitution. They got him on tax evasion. I wonder if we could catch Raymond Pascal Gusarov the same way."

Dr. Mendelson looked as if he'd rather stick leeches all over my face, the way plastic surgeons do, to suck off congested blood in post-surgical muscle flaps.

I licked my lips, but kept going. "You could report him to a collections agency, too, of course, so that you could get your money back. But this man … he posted another photo this morning. See?" I held up my iPhone. He hardly glanced at the picture of a hamster with an ice pick through its heart, pinned to the table while its little paws hung in the air.

Finally, Dr. Mendelson said, "I'm not doing this for you."

My heart dropped in my stomach.

"I'm doing it for someone else." He picked up his phone and started making calls.

A month later, the police dropped by Raymond Pascal Gusarov's apartment and knocked on the door. I'm pretty sure that's not standard in a case of suspected animal abuse and unpaid surgical bills, but Dr. Mendelson must've had better pull with the police than I did.

Gusarov yelled through the door, "Fuck you, pigs."

This did not endear him to the cops, especially when he started banging on the door and saying, "You can't come in here without a warrant. Go away!" and someone in the apartment started to scream.

The police obtained a warrant, lickety-split. They liberated the person in the apartment, a minor held against his will, and dragged Gusarov into their vehicle.

I heard some of it on the news, but Dr. Mendelson filled me on the whole story at his clinic the following day.

"It's bad blood. Bad blood," Dr. Mendelson muttered. He crossed his arms and fell silent while facing the giant picture window overlooking Cote-des-Neiges.

We watched the line of cars at the stoplight and the people zigzagging on the sidewalk, carrying their briefcases and gift bags.

Eventually, I thanked Dr. Mendelson and tiptoed out of his office, barely catching something that he said in Yiddish. I let his secretary usher me out, but before I left their shining office, I asked, over the fresh, pink roses sitting on her desk, "What did he say?"

She pressed her lips together before she told me, "*A shlekhter sholem iz beser vi a guter krig*."

From hanging around with Tucker, I know a teensy bit of German. *Besser* means better, and *krig* sounds a little like *Blitzkrieg*. "What does it mean?"

I could tell she wanted to tell me to shove it, but she glanced at the patient coming in behind me and said, "'A bad peace is better than a good war.' Good day, Dr. Sze."

I turned to face the patient, a man whose grey hair and spotted hands belonged to someone in his sixties, but whose tight face seemed eerily younger. The patient smiled at me with gleaming, white teeth.

THE END

THE HEROES IN THE SHADOWS

THE TRUE STORY BEHIND "THE SIN EATERS"

Part 1

Let me start with a story of a 33-year-old international student. He came to Canada in July of 2011 to study computer engineering at Concordia University. He worked out at the gym four days a week. He didn't smoke, drink, or do drugs. Instead, he worked part-time at a corner store to supplement his income.

He planned to stay in Canada after graduation, enjoying the language, the opportunities, and the fresh air.

His parents were proud of their handsome son's adventurous spirit, and his mother appreciated Canada's reputation for safety. However, they worried because he'd been divorced already, and they wanted him to marry again.

What Jun Lin's parents didn't know was that he was already in relationship with another university student. They'd actually moved to Montreal from China together and shared an apartment. But that student was another man named Feng Lin.

Jun's parents expected him to marry a woman. He broke up with Feng on May 13, 2012, when Feng returned to China for the summer.

Jun joined Grindr to meet other men. Still, Jun and Feng remained close over the next week and a half, texting each other up to 50 or 60 times a day.

On May 24, Jun sent his last text at 9 p.m., wishing Feng Lin a good morning because his friend would be waking up in an opposite time one.

The boss noticed when Jun didn't show up to work the next day.

On the other side of the world, Feng Lin grew increasingly worried. Jun Lin had stopped answering his texts. In fact, it looked like he wasn't even reading them.

Feng Lin asked a friend in Montreal to look for Jun Lin. The friend checked on Jun Lin's apartment on May 27th and found a pan on the stove, eggs on the counter, and a very hungry cat. The friend also tried the university and the convenience store before telling the Chinese consulate that Jun was missing. Jun was reported missing to the police on May 29.

Feng Lin decided to return to Canada on May 30th to search for Jun Lin himself. On a stopover in Qatar, Feng Lin heard that the police had found a torso in a suitcase, but he thought that was unrelated.

When Feng Lin landed, though, he heard that it was Jun Lin.

Part 2

[Trigger warning: not for the squeamish or anyone with a sensitive soul.]

On May 15, 2012, someone began promoting a video called *1 Lunatic 1 Ice Pick.*

Ten days later, on May 25, someone uploaded the promised video. *1 Lunatic 1 Ice Pick* showed a naked man tied to a bed, tortured with an ice pick and a kitchen knife. At some point, part of his body was cut off with a knife and fork. A dog was encouraged to chew on his remains. Necrophilia occurred.

Some viewers reported the video, including a lawyer from Montana who alerted his local sheriff, the Toronto Police, and the Federal Bureau of Investigation. They all ignored him.

Also on May 25th, a building superintendent noted a suitcase in an alleyway behind an apartment building. It had been set out for trash. It wasn't collected because the collectors had too much garbage that week.

On May 29th, three things happened.

The Conservative Part of Canada received a bloody, foul-smelling package in the mail on May 29th. It contained a severed left foot.

Canada Post intercepted a package for the Liberal Party. It contained a left hand.

And hours before the other two events, the building superintendent and another man decided to open the suitcase still lying in the alley. They discovered Jun Lin's torso, covered in maggots.

Part 3

This case haunted me.

Not only did it take place in my old stomping ground in Montreal, Côte-des-Neiges, but the brutality constantly whispered through the back of my mind.

I researched the murderer, whom I am choosing not to name. I'm following the lead of New Zealand prime minister Jacinda Ardern, who will not name the Christchurch shooter, denying him the notoriety he craved.

"The Butcher of Montreal" sought out plastic surgery, spread rumours that he was in a relationship with serial killer Karla Homolka, started at least 70 pages on Facebook, and auditioned for reality TV shows. So he is, at the very least, a narcissist.

However, for "The Sin Eaters," I decided to follow how they uncovered the murderer's identity.

Had I written a police procedural based on real events, I would have written this story instead:

The building superintendent, Michael Nadeau, called 911 on May 29th.

One police officer, Peter D'Avola, was the first to enter what was subsequently determined to be the killer's apartment. D'Avola already knew the building, having previously fielded over ten different calls for drug and alcohol-related complaints. He searched for the perpetrator or a victim, but the apartment was mostly empty, apart from "strong chemical smell, mixed a bit with the smell of a cadaver."

Antonio Paradiso, the homicide detective, interviewed the building superintendent and the building manager. Paradiso began reviewing the building's surveillance cameras for an hour before the news broke of the foot in Ottawa.

Meanwhile, the lead investigator, Claudette Hamlin, had her team of officers assess that pile of garbage waiting for pickup.

In the garbage, they found human limbs and a dead puppy. They also found knives, a circular saw, a hammer, and bloody clothes. They noted electronics, packaging material, and a piece of identification for the killer, which made them wonder if he could possibly be the victim rather than the perpetrator.

By 22:05, the officers called it a night—until they heard about the snuff film that had been posted online. Police officers recognized the Casablanca poster and the wine bottle in the background of *1 Lunatic 1 Ice Pick*.

They hurried back to the garbage bags in the alley and retrieved these items. Later, they were able to extract DNA from both of them.

Officers showed surveillance camera footage to the building manager. One man kept walking in and out of the building on May 25 and 26, emptying his apartment. The building manager identified that man.

The post office's cameras had also captured the killer's face, which matched the ID he'd left in the garbage along with some of his victim's remains, the puppy's body, and the tools of torture and dismemberment.

Now they knew the killer's identity. Unfortunately, the killer had already hopped a flight to Paris May 26th. There, the killer spent hours on GayRomeo.com, talking with a German man in his 50's, who invited the killer to join him in Berlin.

The killer took the bus to Berlin on May 31st. They partied together in bars and brothels and hung out with friends. However, the German had work to do on June 4th, so he sent the killer to an Internet café.

On his commute to work, the German bought a newspaper with a picture of the killer and a description of the crimes.

The German called the police.

Meanwhile, the man who worked in the Internet café's tobacco shop, Kadir Anlayisli, recognized the killer.

Anlayisli ran into the street and flagged down a police officer, who didn't believe him. Anlayisli had to get the attention of a second police car. The second officer called for backup.

In the end, seven officers entered the Internet café and found the killer reading stories about himself online. Initially, he denied it, but the in the end, he admitted, "You got me."

Over $375,000 later, he was extradited to Canada for trial. If he'd fought the extradition, or if he'd committed more crimes in Germany, it would have dragged out longer. I suppose we should be grateful that he came relatively quietly.

Part 4

Reading this stories now, I have a lot of questions. I heard some of these details at the time, but not all of them.

You'll notice that we could have caught him sooner. The lawyer reporting the snuff film was ignored by three different entities, and the tobacco shop worker was dismissed at first.

Laziness gave us a break: most of the evidence would have been thrown in a landfill site if Montreal's garbage collection was more organized.

I wonder if the dead puppy was the same dog as in his horrific snuff film.

How much did Jun suffer? You may need to avert your eyes for this: his throat was slashed while he was still alive. He was stabbed 37 times in the chest and 18 in the abdomen. The pathologist thinks that the killer took a hammer to Jun because the fractures were "too many ... to be counted." They only found his head the following month, after an anonymous tip by fax through a Toronto lawyer. The only mercy was that the forensic toxicologist found Benadryl and Temazepam in Jun's blood, both of which can be used as sleeping pills. Temazepam can be ordered over the Internet to sedate victims before sexual assault or homicide.

I was furious that the defence lawyer for the killer, Luc Leclair, maligned Jun Lin. He painted the victim as promiscuous because he used Grindr. The lawyer forced Feng Lin to watch stills from pornographic videos on Jun's computer and showed him chats that suggested Jun had sexual relations with other men after their breakup.

Just goes to show that, as recently as 2012, in a supposedly progressive country like Canada, your sexual history will be used against you, even if you're the victim of torture and murder, as shown on video.

Feng Lin kept his cool. "We had split up all that time already so he had all his freedom," he replied. When the lawyer forced him to watch the most explicit stills from a porn video on Jun's computer, Feng asked if this was necessary. Feng's lawyer objected and the line of questioning was dropped.

Feng's a hero. We have a lot of heroes in this story. It's important to remember that. Feng flew all the way from China to check on his ex-boyfriend. He withstood the smear campaign by the defence lawyer.

Part 5

For my short story, I had to concentrate on a smaller piece of the puzzle. I knew I wouldn't chronicle a police investigation and trial in a few thousand words unless I left large gaps.

The killer's affinity for plastic surgery could make him

cross paths with Dr. Hope Sze, but how would she end up suspecting him and collecting evidence against him?

As I kept delving into the real killer's past, I found that he had posted videos torturing cats in 2010, including "1 boy 2 kittens," where he used a vacuum cleaner to suffocate two kittens.

Animal rights groups reported him and eventually used photo evidence to identify him.

And so "The Sin Eaters" was born.

Has the killer been punished? He was convicted on all counts: first-degree murder, offering indignities to a human body, distributing obscene materials, using the postal service to distribute obscene materials, and criminal harassment. This means life in prison for at least 25 years. He was sentenced to another 19 years for other charges, but these will be served concurrently.

Meanwhile, the media reports that the killer is literally sun tanning in prison and enjoys rocking out to Céline Dion. In 2015, he posted an ad on a dating website, seeking a "single white male, 28-38 years of age, white and in shape."

Gosh, I think maybe he wants someone white.

The ad also requests "One who is loyal, preferably educated, financially and emotionally stable for a long-term committed relationship. If you think you could be my prince charming, send me a detailed letter with at least 2 photos." Oh, so you'd better be rich, good-looking, and able to keep it zipped. But don't forget white!

I'm applying extra sarcasm because apparently the killer had previously posted racist B.S. on the hate site Stormfront, including how much he hates Chinese people.

In 2017, the killer married a fellow inmate.

Now, I'm someone who thinks we should try to rehabilitate if possible. I've also moved away from supporting the death penalty, which, in addition to ethical concerns, has been shown to cost the state more because of all the trials. However, I can't see how this particular killer has developed a conscience or an ounce of compassion.

If I concentrated on this injustice, it would eat me alive.

I truly hope Jun Lin didn't suffer too much. I haven't watched the snuff film, but I heard he didn't move much, so I pray that he was drugged or unconscious during the torture.

Jun's mother and sister were so devastated that they couldn't work. They both tried to attend the preliminary hearings, but in the end, neither of them felt capable of approaching the courthouse, let alone entering the building day after day. They ended up flying back to China.

Jun's father, Diran Lin, came every day. He wanted to honour his son by bearing witness. He kept silent until the victim's impact statement. I'll note that in China, you put the surname first (Lin, in this case), because the clan is more important than the individual.

> *My brave son, smart son, laughing son, caring son, adventurous son, handsome son, strong son, popular son. Gone. And I will always miss you Lin Jun....*
>
> *I am told that the accused will receive the maximum under Canadian judicial system for one of his crimes....*
>
> *I am also told that for the next years, a prisoner will be housed, his bed provided, his food prepared, doctors made available and psychiatrists to listen to him and give him medication when he tells them that he feels bad.*
>
> *No one will house us, feed us or provide doctors. Lin Jun will never be there for us. We do not want to tell our story because it is too sad to repeat. We cannot talk much about Lin Jun without talking about his murder. The murder has robbed*

us not only of Lin Jun but our ability to think and talk about him without feeling pain and shame.

Part 6

"The Sin Eaters" was originally published in *Montreal Noir* and was shortlisted for the Arthur Ellis Award for the best crime story in Canada.

Sometimes, people ask me to define noir as a genre. I've heard three definitions, but I only remember one: things spiral and get more and more fucked up.

Overall, my stories usually end on a high note, although my friend, the author Richard Quarry, noticed that the last line may contain a scorpion sting.

In this case, real life is more noir than my fiction.

However, I try to remember a few things. One, that killer is a narcissist. He wants us to pay attention to him. He believes he's superior. Even if he's getting ass-raped with a broken light bulb, he'll pretend it was all part of his grand country club prison plan. Sure, the media reports his life of ease, but outrage sells. Anger is clickbait.

From what I've heard, prison is mostly boring and involves being treated like cattle, constantly penned and shuffled from one place to another with no autonomy. The killer would loathe that.

The other thing I remember are the quiet heroes. They didn't grab the headlines, but they did the right thing.

The lawyer and other viewers who reported the snuff film.

The building superintendent who unzipped that suitcase. It must have smelled horrific after three days, but he and his friend uncovered the main evidence, and the superintendent was able to identify the killer on surveillance video.

The police officers who put boots on the ground, entering that building, studying a snuff film that no one should have to witness, and physically cataloguing each heartbreaking, terrifying piece of evidence. The second Berlin officer who called for backup and called in the cavalry. And every officer in between who listened, on both sides of the Atlantic.

The tobacco seller/café employee who recognized the killer and wouldn't take one police officer's no for an answer.

The media who reported the killer's crimes.

The animal rights activists who started the campaign to unmask the killer two years prior.

The Concordia students who raised money for Jun's family. You can still donate money at http://www.linjunfamily.com.

The friend who searched everywhere for Jun.

The Crown attorney, the judge, and the translators at the trial. The jury who convicted the killer.

Jun's family. His mother couldn't work, which is the next thing to death for an Asian person, but she didn't kill herself. She chose to face the agony of a world without her beautiful son. The same son who seemed to break up with an honourable man because of his parents' disapproval, and who died eleven days later. Which might make Jun's parents blame themselves.

Jun's sister, who stopped working because she was trying to support her mother and hold herself together. I hope she has the time and energy to mourn too.

Jun's father, who stayed strong for his remaining family throughout this ordeal. Mr. Lin stayed silent during the trial until the victim impact statement. I don't know how he has broken inside, but he maintained his dignity. In Asian culture, saving face is very important. But his full victim impact statement says everything.

And most of all, I think of Feng Lin, who loved Jun so much that he was looking out for him from the opposite side of the globe. They texted constantly. Even though Jun had broken up with him. Even though Jun was hooking up with other guys. Jun had said he needed to marry a woman for his parents, but he did seem to make full use of his freedom, which must have pained Feng.

Despite that, when Jun stopped texting him or reading his messages, Feng leaped into action. He contacted a friend who searched everywhere in vain. Then Feng decided *No, I'm going to fly in myself. I don't care if we're not together anymore. It doesn't matter if I'm working on the other side of the planet. I love him. I've got to find him.*

Feng was too late. But he did his utmost. And he came back to testify at the trial, outing himself as both a gay man and the man who was cast aside.

To give you a sample of China's attitude toward homosexuality, from 1979 to 1997, it was officially deemed a form of "hooliganism," meaning a threat to society "treatable" with "re-education" *(gai zao)*. So even in 2012, coming out would probably tank Feng's job and social status in China.

Not that Canada would seem any better, with the defence lawyer painting Jun as an S&M manslut and Feng as a blind fool. In the 21st century, I have no idea why this would be considered relevant or admissible in court, but these accusations must have wounded Feng, the implication that Jun had broken up with him in order to sleep around.

Remember what I said about saving face? For Feng to admit he's gay, to admit that Jun broke up with him, to take the stand while the defence lawyer tries to humiliate Feng and insult Jun post-death—it's career and social suicide, both here and in China.

Feng withstood it in order to convict the killer who tortured, killed, defiled, and dismembered the man he loved.

Feng Lin. Now that's a fucking hero.

When I name the heroes, they far outnumber the killer and his aficionados.

Be careful when you admire the powerful and the ruthless. As Aldous Huxley pointed out, "So long as men worship the Caesars and Napoleons, Caesars and Napoleons will duly rise and make them miserable."

In the midst of hell, we have to remember the heroes in the shadows. The Dalai Lama has commented that bad news makes headlines because it's unusual. Good people don't necessarily make headlines. They quietly make things right without expecting praise or applause.

> I think a hero is any person really intent on making this a better place for all people.
>
> *Maya Angelou*

> We do not have to become heroes overnight. Just a step at a time, meeting each thing that comes up ... discovering we have the strength to stare it down.
>
> *Eleanor Roosevelt*

AFTERWORD

That was a tough essay. Sometimes they ask if crime writing is ethical because we glorify violence, but I try to gaze into the belly of the beast in order to prevent more beasts.

In case anyone is wondering, that's not Hope on the cover. It's not the killer, Tucker, or Ryan either. I don't believe "whitewashing" covers (using white models to represent characters of colour), but I thought this photo symbolized the noir spirit and the idea of sin eaters in our society rather than a literal representation of our heroes.

Thanks for reading.

Thanks for leaving a review.

Thanks for joining my mailing list at **www.melissayuaninnes.com** and getting a free novella.

Thanks for saying hi on social media.

See you in Egypt for Hope Sze #8. Yup, Hope's going to Cairo.

Join Melissa's mailing list at www.melissayuaninnes.com

ABOUT THE AUTHOR

Melissa Yi is the pseudonym for an emergency physician and a proud finalist for the Arthur Ellis Award (best crime story in Canada) and the Derringer Award (best mystery story in the English language).

Get a free Hope novella by joining the KamikaSze newsletter on Melissa's website, www.myi.ninja

Leaving a positive review online helps authors grow.

facebook.com/MelissaYiYuanInnes
twitter.com/dr_sassy
bookbub.com/authors/melissa-yi
instagram.com/melissa.yuaninnes
pinterest.com/melissayi_
amazon.com/author/myi

ALSO BY MELISSA YI

Code Blues (Hope Sze 1)

Notorious D.O.C. (Hope Sze 2)

Family Medicine (essay & Hope Sze novella combining the short stories *Cain and Abel, Trouble and Strife, and Butcher's Hook*, which are also available separately)

Terminally Ill (Hope Sze 3)

Student Body (Hope Sze novella post-Terminally Ill; includes radio drama *No Air*)

Blood Diamonds (Hope Sze short story)

The Sin Eaters (Hope Sze short story)

Stockholm Syndrome (Hope Sze 4)

Human Remains (Hope Sze 5)

Blue Christmas (Hope Sze short story)

Death Flight (Hope Sze 6)

Graveyard Shift (Hope Sze 7)

Scorpion Scheme (Hope Sze 8, coming December 2020)

More mystery & romance novels by Melissa Yi

The Italian School for Assassins *(Octavia & Dario Killer School Mystery 1)*

The Goa Yoga School of Slayers *(Octavia & Dario Killer School Mystery 2)*

Wolf Ice

High School Hit List

The List

Dancing Through the Chaos

Unfeeling Doctor Series (Melissa Yuan-Innes)

The Most Unfeeling Doctor in the World and Other True Tales From the Emergency Room (Unfeeling Doctor #1)

The Unfeeling Doctor, Unplugged: More True Tales From Med School and Beyond (Unfeeling Doctor #2)

The Unfeeling Wannabe Surgeon: A Doctor's Medical School Memoir (Unfeeling Doctor #3)

The Unfeeling Thousandaire: How I Made $10,000 Indie Publishing and You Can, Too! (Unfeeling Doctor #4)

Buddhish: Exploring Buddhism in a Time of Grief: One Doctor's Story (Unfeeling Doctor #5)

The Unfeeling Doctor Betwixt Birthing Babies: Poems About Love, Loss, and More Love (Unfeeling Doctor #6)

The Knowledgeable Lion: Poems and Prose by the Unfeeling Doctor in Africa (Unfeeling Doctor #7)

Fifty Shades of Grey's Anatomy: The Unfeeling Doctor's Fresh Confessions from the Emergency Room (Unfeeling Doctor #8)

Broken Bones: New True Noir Essays From the Emergency Room by the Most Unfeeling Doctor in the World (Unfeeling Doctor #9)

The Emergency Doctor's Guide Series (Melissa Yuan-Innes)

The Emergency Doctor's Guide to a Pain-Free Back: Fast Tips and Exercises for Healing and Relief

The Emergency Doctor's Guide to Healing Dry Eyes

www.ingramcontent.com/pod-product-compliance
Lightning Source LLC
La Vergne TN
LVHW051022080826
845145LV00009B/2750